"It's Not About The Money. It's About My Dad's Legacy. I'll Prove Tarrant Forced My Father Into Selling Against His Will And Then The Courts Will Restore His Work To My Family."

Alarm mixed with amusement made him snort. "You're going to sue Hardcastle Enterprises?"

Bella held Dominic's gaze, her gray eyes unblinking. "Yes. I know a judge will do the right thing."

"Sounds to me like you have way too much faith in the legal system and not nearly enough in Tarrant's utter ruthlessness. Did you find what you need?"

"Not yet. Are you going to have me fired?"

"Me? Oh, yeah, the son and heir. I don't know what the hell I'm going to do with you...."

Except kiss you again, maybe....

Dear Reader,

Incredible advances have been made in DNA research, allowing individuals to map their ancestry back hundreds of years. Genetic analysis can now prove that people are related, even if they were totally unaware of a connection. This potential for the sudden discovery of new family members generated the idea for my three-book THE HARDCASTLE PROGENY series, in which dying billionaire Tarrant Hardcastle goes looking for heirs among the illegitimate children he once scorned.

In this first story, Tarrant approaches Dominic DiBari, who he'd previously insisted—in court—wasn't his. What would it be like to suddenly have your world turned upside down by the appearance of the father who once spurned you? And then to find yourself falling in love with a woman who is that father's sworn enemy?

It was interesting to explore the confusion and emotion inherent in the situation, and I hope you enjoy Dominic and Bella's whirlwind romance.

Jen

JENNIFER LEWIS

MILLIONAIRE'S SECRET SEDUCTION

Published by Silhouette Books
America's Publisher of Contemporary Romance

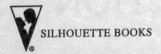

SILHOUETTE BOOKS

ISBN-13: 978-0-373-76925-4
ISBN-10: 0-373-76925-3

Recycling programs
for this product may
not exist in your area.

MILLIONAIRE'S SECRET SEDUCTION

Visit Silhouette Books at www.eHarlequin.com

Printed in U.S.A.

Books by Jennifer Lewis

Silhouette Desire

The Boss's Demand #1812
Seduced for the Inheritance #1830
Black Sheep Billionaire #1847
Prince of Midtown #1891
*Millionaire's Secret Seduction #1925

*The Hardcastle Progeny

JENNIFER LEWIS

has been dreaming up stories for as long as she can remember, and is thrilled to be able to share them with readers. She has lived on both sides of the Atlantic and worked in media and the arts before she grew bold enough to put pen to paper. Happily settled in New York with her family, she would love to hear from readers at jen@jen-lewis.com.

For my children,
who are my inspiration in every possible way.

Acknowledgment

Grateful thanks to those who read this story
while I wrote it, including Amanda, Anne,
Anne-Marie, Betty, Carol, Cynthia, Leeanne,
Marie, Mel and Paula, and my agent Andrea.
And for the true genius behind Trader Joes. Even if the
curried chickpeas never come back, you're a true hero.

One

"Get out before I call security!"

The woman's voice rang across the large space. Dominic Di Bari blinked in the fierce light that poured through a wall of windows.

Apparently she had no idea who he was. He took a step forward.

"I said—"

"I heard what you said." He could just make out a figure at the far end of the room, small in the cavernous space. "I don't believe we've met."

"The sales training conference is on fourteen. This is fifteen." She strode toward him, heels clicking on the marble.

He squinted, but still couldn't see much. She had a white lab coat on. Computers and other high tech equipment punctuated long countertops. A white marble floor magnified the late-afternoon sunlight blasting through the windows.

"Is this some kind of lab?"

"I hardly see that it's any of your business."

"A week ago, I'd have agreed with you." Before the strange phone call that turned his life upside down.

"I warned you I'd have to call security." She pulled a phone from a pocket in her lab coat. He couldn't help but notice that her legs went on forever. She dialed the number and tapped her foot on the floor, looking anywhere but at him.

He crossed his arms and fought a smile that kept trying to sneak across his mouth. Judging from those legs, he'd bet there was quite a body hidden under all that white permanent-press polyester. Straight brown hair with natural-looking gold highlights grazed her shoulder as she pressed the phone to her ear.

"Yes, Sylvester, there's an intruder on fifteen. I told him to leave but he won't." She shot him a hostile glance. Gray eyes. "Thank you, I'd appreciate that."

She snapped her phone shut. "Security will be here in a few moments. Now is your chance to exit with dignity."

"Dignity can be so dull." He leaned against the doorframe. Her anger lit her cool eyes and hardened the determined set of her chin. "Are you a researcher here?" he asked.

"As it happens, I'm an executive vice president in the cosmetics division." She pursed her lips.

"Interesting." So Tarrant's eye for the ladies extended to those he picked to run his company. This woman didn't look a day over twenty-five. Obviously legs trumped experience around here. Hardly surprising, given what he knew about Tarrant Hardcastle, the jerk that DNA tests had proved to be his biological father.

He heard an elevator open behind him.

"This is him." She pointed a long, graceful finger at him.

No nail polish. Shouldn't she be wearing some if she was EVP of cosmetics?

"Mr. Hardcastle." The friendly middle-aged security chief who'd been instructed to give him the run of the building gave a little nod.

Dominic knew he should correct him. He'd been Dominic Di Bari his whole life and he had no intention of changing his name now to suit some egomaniacal billionaire who needed an instant son.

But right now being Mr. Hardcastle suited his purposes.

Her pretty pink lips parted. "What?"

"You heard the man." Dominic shifted his weight. "Sylvester, is there a problem?"

"Ms. Andrews mentioned an intruder."

"I think there's been some mistake." Dominic spoke slowly, and let that smile he'd been fighting pull his mouth upward. "Dominic." He held out his hand for her to shake.

She stared at it in horror. Then she stepped forward and shook it. "Bella Andrews. I had no idea. I must apologize. We deal with a lot of sensitive material in this lab and we can't have strangers…" She trailed off.

"I quite understand." Her skin was soft and smooth—as it should be, given her chosen profession. Her palm heated against his as he held her hand a couple of beats longer than was truly polite.

Her gray eyes gave away nothing of her thoughts.

When he let go she pulled her hand back fast and turned to the security guy. "Thanks, Sylvester. Sorry to have bothered you."

They stood in silence while Sylvester made his exit. He could almost feel her burning curiosity as a palpable force in the chemical-scented air. He smiled, as if to invite her most probing questions.

"You're one of Tarrant's relatives?" Her skin colored after she asked.

"His son." He gave her a cool smile. "You're going to say you didn't know he had a son, aren't you?"

"I, um." She pushed a stray wisp of hair behind her ear.

The story wasn't a pretty one, and he decided to keep it to himself for now. Sometimes it was fun to keep people guessing. Especially a scientist who probably lived to have her hypotheses proven correct.

"My father invited me here to show me how the company works." He took a step toward her. "So, to repeat my question, is this a lab?"

"Yes, it's the development lab." He watched her elegant fingers brush a speck of imaginary dust from a computer monitor. "I must apologize again. I hope you realize that I'm just protecting the company's interests."

"I understand. The fountain of eternal youth must be safeguarded at all costs."

His eyes had adjusted to the light and he could see the end of the long room. The sinks and burners he might have expected in a lab were there, carefully separated from racks of computing equipment and other robotic-looking devices. He didn't see any beakers or test tubes. Those must be hidden in the expensive cabinets lining the far wall. "Let me guess, you're really seventy-eight years old?"

A dimple pierced the smooth skin of her cheek. "Not quite. Though we've made some impressive advances in antiaging products. Do you have experience in the field?"

She shoved her hands in her pockets, which had the delightful effect of pulling her lab coat tight over her shapely backside as she crossed the lab.

"Not a lick, I'm afraid. I'm here to learn."

To learn as much as he could about Tarrant Hardcastle and his evil empire, where until a week ago he'd been very unwelcome.

Dominic still smarted over losing his bid for the bankrupt chain of drugstores he'd counted on as real estate for his chain of food stores. Tarrant had undercut him on the price and still got them. Now every store was sitting boarded up—a blight on the main drag of at least fifty towns in America.

Did Tarrant know he'd screwed over his own son? Had he done it deliberately, as a kind of power play?

Just thinking about it heated Dominic's blood. But he'd get his own back, one way or another.

Bella Andrews gathered some papers that were spread out on a counter and shoved them into a drawer. Her breathing shallow, she looked nervous.

And maybe she should be. Her high-handed attitude—and the way those luscious lips pressed together in a line of disapproval—gave him an appetite for a little sweet revenge.

She had to get rid of him. Thank God he didn't get a look at the files she'd been reading. The entire team of research chemists was at a conference in Geneva and she'd been sure of some privacy for serious snooping. Now she'd almost been caught red-handed by the boss's son.

Tarrant Hardcastle had a son?

"This is where our staff of chemists experiments with new formulas and improves on the current ones. We have a strict chain of procedures and each product is thoroughly tested before it hits the market."

"On animals?" His eyebrow raised.

Funny question. Despite his elegant suit, Tall, Dark and Dangerous looked like a man more likely to eat animals raw than to worry about their welfare.

"We eliminated animal testing when I arrived. It's not necessary for our products." She sucked in a breath. "Right now we're working on a new line of age-defying cosmetics. In fact, our first product launches in a few days. Tarrant hopes to secure global distribution by the end of the year."

"I don't doubt he'll succeed." Something in his tone made her glance up. His black-coffee eyes locked onto hers. "Do you like working for Hardcastle Enterprises?"

"Of course, why?" Her voice came out kind of squeaky. It sometimes did that when she was lying.

And something about this man put her on edge. Not his *L'Uomo Vogue* good looks. She was used to that. Tarrant Hardcastle put a premium on pretty faces—male and female—in his employees.

Nor was it the tall, broad-shouldered frame lounging against the marble counter.

There was something in his expression that gave her the idea he could see right through her. A possibility that made her belly contract with anxiety.

"Just curious."

The look of satisfaction on his face suggested he'd read her traitorous thoughts. Her gut tightened into a knot, even though she knew that was impossible. "What would you like to see?"

His dark gaze drifted across the front of her lab coat, implying that his answer was "more of you." "So far I've only seen the inside of corporate offices and conference rooms. I'd like to see the lab, then…" He tilted his head and narrowed his eyes. Was he laughing at her? "If you can take some time from your busy schedule, I'd like to see the retail floors."

Of course she had time. All her other plans were irrelevant if the boss's "son" needed her. Couldn't he find someone in retail for that? He was definitely laughing at her. Now that she'd insulted him by trying to throw him out, he was going to toy with her like a cat with freshly trapped prey. Irritation prickled over her—along with something else she couldn't put her finger on.

She crossed the room, conscious of his big body keeping close to her. "This is a photon microscope." She gestured at her pride and joy. "We're working with microfine powders that can reflect light to create the illusion of optical smoothness."

Instead of glazing over, his eyes fixed on hers. "Nanotechnology."

A spark of surprise leapt inside her. "Yes. We've found that by manipulating photons in layers we can create dramatic effects with both colors and surfaces."

"Fascinating." He ran a big thumb over the top of a microscope, which caused a disturbing ripple of sensation in her belly. "And you've created a marketable product?"

"I can see you understand the business. Our biggest challenge wasn't finding something that worked, it was making it marketable. People won't buy a cake of white powder just because they're told it's a great red lipstick that never bleeds and won't wear off. We've come up with a compound we're calling ReNew, because it makes damaged skin look new again."

"Are you a chemist?" His eyes drifted over her lab coat again. Made it feel hot against her skin.

She lifted her chin. "I have degrees in chemistry and business. I'm here to lead the team." *And take back my father's stolen legacy.*

Tarrant Hardcastle would never give her dad a word of credit, even if his life's work made millions for the company. They had no idea she was his daughter. If Tarrant found out he'd probably fire her.

She needed to get this new Hardcastle out of her lab, and

now. She'd been surprised in the middle of her unofficial "research" and didn't want Tarrant's son poking around and jumping to any conclusions.

She started to unbutton her lab coat. "You wanted to see the public areas. Shall we start with the department store?"

He seemed distracted by her fingers on the buttons. When his eyes lifted to meet hers they were darker than ever. "Sure."

His voice was low, suggestive.

He hung behind her as they walked out of the lab and she could feel his gaze on her. Her fitted, dark red skirt and blouse had been chosen to curry favor with her boss, Tarrant Hardcastle—lover of all things expensive and feminine. Making an effort to look good was part of the unofficial job requirements around here. Apparently she'd succeeded, because she sensed Dominic Hardcastle's approval radiating like a heat wave.

She hung her lab coat on a hook by the door, ushered him out then locked the door behind her.

Phew.

The tour didn't require much travel, since Tarrant was such a megalomaniac and control freak that he had gathered his entire empire under the slate mansard roof of a former hotel, a robber-baron-era extravaganza overlooking the southern tip of Central Park. The palatial building contained the corporate offices, conference rooms and auditoriums, the lab, a private art gallery, three glittering retail floors and a world-class restaurant on the top floor.

Costly fragrances hung in the air as they stepped out of the elevator on the ground-level retail floor. Hardcastle's exclusive products took pride of place among Chanel, Dior, et al, in the cosmetics department. Bella watched Dominic stride unselfconsciously past counters laden with seventy-dollar lipsticks and "miracle" skin-renewing potions.

His easy chatter with retail associates demonstrated an insider knowledge of the business. It also revealed total ignorance about cosmetics—or was that feigned to encourage more blushing and fluttering explanations from the stunning girls behind the counters? He even let one raven-haired goddess spray him with the latest unisex Calvin Klein scent. Bella resisted the urge to roll her eyes.

"Where are you going so fast?" A big hand closed around her upper arm as she tried to march onward. Heat gathered under the silk of her blouse.

She eased her arm out of his grasp. "There's a lot to see."

"Indeed there is. Can you blame me for wanting to take my time to enjoy the view?" His face revealed a raised eyebrow and a twinkle of humor. Though his eyes were on her face she had a distinct impression he was appraising her body.

She lifted her chin. "It's nearly seven o'clock and I imagine you'll want to at least see the couture and designer collections on our women's apparel floors."

"Not really." He continued to smile pleasantly. "I had something else in mind."

For a second she thought his voice was thick with suggestion, then she decided she must have imagined it.

"What, exactly?" Her voice sounded clipped.

"Food."

"Oh." She distracted herself from his hungry stare by brushing a tiny piece of white lint from her sleeve. "Is that your specialty as a retailer?" She was following the usual lawyer's advice to never ask a question unless you knew the answer. Several associates had gushed over his chain of food stores.

"In fact it is, but I was thinking dinner."

She blinked rapidly. Did he expect *her* to have dinner with him? She needed to get back to the lab and put those files away.

"I think you owe me, don't you? You did try to get me thrown out of the building."

He cocked his head and let his gaze drift over her mouth. The mouth that had called security to eject the boss's son.

She swallowed.

"I hear The Moon is quite the place to be."

"Oh yes. Five stars," she murmured. She'd read the reviews but had never been there. Way out of her price range.

"Tarr—my *father* told me to be sure to eat dinner there, on his tab." Something about the way he said the word *father* made her ears prick up. His tone had a guarded quality that surprised her. "It would be my pleasure if you'd join me."

His expression looked entirely genuine, and warmth shone in his dark eyes.

She blinked as part of her brain demanded that she agree without hesitation and another more sensible part told her to make up a good excuse, and quick.

"Um, gosh." She checked her watch while she racked her mind for a way out. *It's my hair-washing night?* "Sure, I'd love to." She forced a smile.

It was an interesting experience, walking beside him through retail floors, amid the glamorous, well-heeled shoppers. Every female eye swiveled to Dominic, drinking him in, from his slightly unruly black hair to his black wingtip shoes. After about forty-five seconds Bella began to feel like a cheap handbag draped over the arm of a couture-dressed model.

There was definitely such a thing as being too good-looking, she reflected, as another beauty narrowed her heavily made-up eyes at Dominic Hardcastle. The chiseled jaw, the I-just-got-back-from-the-Caribbean tan that no doubt extended well underneath his custom-tailored suit.

It was all a bit too much.

Vulgar, even. Like so many aspects of his father's glittering retail empire.

"The Moon is on the top floor." She pressed the button. Tried not to notice how his big body filled the tight space of the private staff elevator. "Do you live in New York?"

"Miami. But I might move up here. I'm doing a lot of business in the city these days. And Tarr—my *dad* wants me to be close to headquarters."

Again, the word *dad* had a forced quality that intrigued her. She knew Tarrant had a daughter, but she'd never heard that he had a son. With security expert Sylvester—who she knew had been with Tarrant since before she was born—to vouch for him, she knew he must be the genuine article, but why had he suddenly appeared out of nowhere?

She couldn't help herself. "I don't mean to pry, but I didn't know Tarrant had a son." There, she'd said it. And it was at least fractionally more polite than asking "who the heck are you, anyway?"

"I'm a love child."

Her gaze jerked to his face. Again that hint of humor simmered in the muscles under his skin. Was he mocking her?

"Tarrant had a fling with my mom back in the seventies. They met on the dance floor at Studio 54."

"The disco scene." She'd heard Tarrant had a reputation as the most die-hard partier of the twentieth century.

"At that time he wasn't so interested in the responsibilities of fatherhood." His jaw tightened. "But lately it seems he's had a change of heart."

Silence thickened the air.

Ping. The sound of the doors opening was possibly the best music she'd heard all year.

Had this total stranger just admitted to her that he was Tarrant Hardcastle's unwanted bastard son? His oddly intimate confession gave her a strange feeling.

The restaurant was already packed. The wait for reservations had been at least six months since it opened two years earlier.

"Dominic Hardcastle."

She thought she saw a muscle twitch in his cheek as he said his own name. *Curiouser and curiouser.*

"Welcome, sir. I'll seat you at Mr. Hardcastle's table." The maître d' beamed as Dominic congratulated him on the restaurant's success and they shared some shoptalk on the way to the table. Did everyone fall at this guy's feet?

The décor was extravagantly minimalist; a single, perfect banana leaf in a slim black vase was the only centerpiece on each table.

Dominic pulled out a sleek metal chair, then slid it under her as she sat. Of course he'd have to be a perfect gentleman too.

She shook out her napkin. "I guess it's too early for the moon to make an appearance. The ceiling rolls back to reveal the night sky."

Dominic looked up. She ignored the muscularity of his neck as it strained his perfectly fitted shirt collar. "Can't say I'm sorry. I'm not sure I'd want to worry about an owl swooping down to share my filet mignon." His grin revealed even, white teeth.

"Oh, you don't have to fret about that. Or mosquitoes. There's a curved layer of microfine molded plastic to keep intruders out. If you look carefully you can see where it joins the support columns. All part of the design conception."

Dominic stared at the ceiling with undisguised fascination. "Amazing. Tarrant Hardcastle certainly is a genius, no matter what else you might say about him." He opened his napkin. "Shall we order champagne?"

The barb about Tarrant left her temporarily speechless. Was he testing her somehow? "Sure, champagne sounds great."

"You'll have to tell me what food to choose, since I'm the new kid on the block."

That boyish grin again.

It was a shame she had no idea what was on the menu. "It's all good. That's why people are willing to sell their soul to get a table."

Lucky thing she had an invite. She'd probably already parted with her soul working at Hardcastle Enterprises for an entire year. That she was doing it with a hidden agenda made it a certainty.

The poker-faced waiter handed them each a banana leaf with the night's dishes handwritten on it.

Dominic studied it for a moment, then started to laugh. "I feel bad for the guy back there with the Sharpie."

"Sharpie? He's probably grinding raw pigment to make the ink and sharpening goose feathers into quills." She couldn't help sharing a chuckle.

Dominic had three dimples. One in each cheek and one in his chin. Not that she liked dimples or anything.

They ordered—for her the pan-seared scallops and roasted quail, and for him raw oysters and steak tartare.

He raised his glass. "A toast. To the loveliest woman in Hardcastle Enterprises."

She narrowed her eyes and fought a blush. Bella! How can you fall for a line as well worn as Tarrant Hardcastle's little black book?

"Flattery will get you everywhere." She raised her glass.

That's what I'm hoping. Dominic took a sip of champagne. Dry and crisp, an excellent choice.

There was something about this woman he couldn't put his finger on. Reading people well—spotting their strengths and flaws and maximizing one while minimizing the other—was the skill that enabled him to grow his company so fast and with so much success.

Bella Andrews had a shield up, and apparently she wasn't going to let it down. Yes, she was out with the boss's son, but he'd attempted to put her at ease by pointing out that his connection to Tarrant was anything but glamorous.

She hadn't relaxed one iota. And that intrigued him.

Her pink lips pressed against her champagne glass as she sipped. Not a trace of lipstick.

"I'm surprised you don't wear cosmetics, given your position." He leaned back in his chair, to better survey the effect of his comment on her beautifully unpainted face.

She blinked. The tips of her mascara-free eyelashes were golden. "They say you should stay away from your own product."

"A good rule for drug dealers. Are your products habit-forming?" He had a feeling that looking at the sharp cupid's bow of her upper lip could be habit-forming.

"I certainly hope so. Repeat business is where we stand to make the most profit."

"Is Hardcastle expanding its retail outlets?" He said it casually. Managed to keep the words *what the hell does Tarrant want with fifty-three bankrupt drugstores?* inside his mouth.

"Not that I know of. Our products sell best in upscale department stores and boutique salons. The price point is too high for mass-market retail. I do know Tarrant wants to find more outlets in China."

"Lack of posh department stores there?"

She shrugged. "I don't know. It's outside my area of expertise."

"Which is?"

"Tarr—er, your father hired me to develop new products. He likes to be on the cutting edge."

"How did he find you?"

She licked her lips, an awkward gesture of hesitation that sent a tongue of heat through his groin. "Um, actually I approached him."

Her shield had just grown thicker. Apparently he was hovering around some kind of danger zone.

Interesting.

"How did you convince him to invest in research? Those photon microscopes couldn't have been cheap." He leaned forward as the waiter deposited her plate. He could almost smell her alarm over the scent of the sautéed scallops. "You must be very convincing."

"I told him he had no choice. The market is changing. Nano-technology makes an entirely different type of cosmetic possible. Smearing cover-up over blemishes will be obsolete once people discover our light-refracting products."

"Maybe you should take it one step further and invent a cloak of invisibility."

She blanched. Her fork stopped in midair on its way to her mouth and her brow furrowed.

Dominic's heart kicked up a notch. "Is that what you're doing?"

She let out a forced laugh. "Of course not." She glanced at her scallop, then popped it in her mouth.

Something was definitely up with this one. Doing something she wasn't supposed to. The question remained whether Tarrant was in on it, or not.

He picked up an oyster shell. Stared right at her while he sipped the cool, slippery creature into his mouth and swallowed it whole.

She didn't blink, but her lips parted. She dragged her eyes away and snatched up her water glass.

"You're young to be in such a position of authority." He sipped his champagne. "You must be smart."

Maybe too smart for the good of the company.

"Oh, I don't know." She shrugged again and her slim shoulders moved inside her silky blouse. The soft fabric slid over the breasts.

"You're no slouch yourself." She speared another scallop. "I overheard you talking to the retail associates about your business. For someone who didn't grow up inside the Hardcastle empire you seem to have done well for yourself."

"I do all right."

Bella watched him knock back another oyster. She blinked as he swallowed it and it slid down his throat.

As she'd guessed in the lab, this man liked his food *raw*. He must enjoy living on the edge. Nothing added an adrenaline rush to a meal like the possibility of an invigorating dose of botulism.

She couldn't let herself be sidetracked by his quietly admiring glances. She had a growing suspicion that if Dominic Hardcastle got the chance, he'd eat her alive. He was the enemy. His father destroyed her father. If he knew what she was up to he'd chew her up and spit her out without a second thought.

She blew out a breath and ate her last scallop.

Funny how just the way a man looked at you could make you feel like...a woman.

She must have been spending too much time in the lab with scientists who got turned on by photons rather than by humans. She dressed to impress every day just to fly under the radar at Hardcastle, and she was used to the cool stares of appraisal that rewarded her efforts. They didn't compare in any way with the raw, earthy appreciation she read in Dominic Hardcastle's gaze.

"How did you get into retail?" she asked, to get her mind off the way his long-lashed eyes heated her skin with their steady regard.

"Necessity." He lifted another oyster shell to his lips and leveled a dark look at her. "I started selling stuff in the playground when I was eight. You see, I had this deadbeat dad who didn't pitch in, so I had to help my mom."

He tipped the oyster into his mouth and gulped it down.

"Touching." She sipped her champagne to distract herself from the movement of his Adam's apple as he swallowed.

"Yeah." His dimples appeared. "Then I got bitten by the capitalist bug. Never looked back. When I was fifteen I convinced my mom to give me my Catholic school fees and let me go to the public school instead. I figured I could turn that cash into enough money to go to college and start my own business."

"And she let you?"

"She wasn't happy about it, but she's never regretted it."

"Guess you make a case for nature over nurture. What made Tarrant track you down after all these years?"

"I'm sure you know he has terminal prostate cancer. He's been given a few months to live and that made him realize you can't take it with you. Apparently he's looking for someone to hand the jeweled scepter to."

Of course she knew. Everyone did. The dilemma of who would inherit his empire had been front-page news since the story of his illness broke.

Not that anyone in the company would dare utter a word about it within these hallowed walls.

But something bugged her. "Doesn't he have a daughter?"

"Yes. Fiona. But she's young. Maybe he thinks she's too inexperienced?"

"Or maybe he wants a male heir?"

Dominic's brows lowered. "He certainly never had any interest in one before. After denying paternity for thirty-two years he's suddenly decided to clutch me to his well-clad bosom."

"He literally *denied* paternity?"

"Yup." Dominic's hard-edged expression didn't falter.

She couldn't even imagine what it would be like to have a parent refuse your existence. Her parents had always been her closest friends in the world.

It hurt so much that her dad was gone. And that her mom was… She took in a deep breath to banish a dangerous surge of emotion. "Did your mother ever try to take him to court?"

"She tried. She wanted to send me to a decent school. She was hoping to get some money to move us to a better neighborhood or pay for private school. Tarrant's lawyers got the case thrown out of court."

"How did they do that?"

His jaw hardened. "It was before DNA. They just laughed off the idea that a big shot like Tarrant Hardcastle would be fooling around with an ordinary girl from Brooklyn, and the judge believed him."

Bella let out a slow breath. "I'd be mad."

Something flickered in his eyes. "Yeah." He picked up his champagne glass and knocked the rest of it back. "Lucky thing I've got better things to worry about, huh?"

"They do say living well is the best revenge."

"Then I guess we're both getting revenge on someone." A crooked smile slid across his lips.

The waiter put plates, artfully arranged with their expensive entrées, in front of them and placed another champagne bottle in the bucket of ice.

If you only knew.

Living well didn't mean a thing if there was a white flame of anger burning inside you. Her father had been so close to fulfilling his dream. After enduring decades of snide laughter from peers and so-called colleagues, he'd finally come within reach of manipulating particles to alter their surface properties.

Even his fantasy of a cloak of invisibility was no longer a laughing matter.

Then Tarrant Hardcastle had bullied him into selling his life's work for a pittance. With his dreams gone, he succumbed to undiagnosed heart disease and was gone within months.

Her chest tightened. She wouldn't wish that death on anyone, not even Tarrant Hardcastle. But she *would* get her father's work back and make his dream come true.

She owed it to him.

A long shadow across the tablecloth jolted her back to reality.

"Dominic!" Two striking women materialized next to him, one on each side. A statuesque redhead in a tight green number bent to kiss his cheek, while an ebony-skinned beauty in a slinky cream sheath grabbed his hand. "You didn't tell us you were coming to town. We'll have to punish you." Her accent sounded French.

Dominic put down his fork, rose and gave each girl an intimate kiss on the cheek. Bella stabbed her innocent quail as a wave of irritation rose in her chest.

Dominic's dimples appeared. "Bella, I'd like you to meet two of my best clients."

Two arms as long as javelins stuck out at her and she shook their perfectly manicured hands. Luckily she managed not to cut herself on the array of sparkling rocks decorating their shapely fingers.

Dominic introduced them and both their names sounded vaguely familiar. Probably former supermodels.

As they towered over her, Bella's contact lenses seemed to morph back into the thick glasses she'd worn as a teen. Her blouse and skirt felt as glamorous as her lab coat. And she'd dared to imagine that Dominic Hardcastle was attracted to *her?*

Must be delusional.

She shoved a stray strand of hair off her forehead. "Nice to meet you. Dominic asked me to show him around Hardcastle Enterprises. He wanted to try the restaurant." She blushed, suddenly feeling pathetic that she had to explain what a man like Dominic would be doing in an expensive restaurant with a nondescript scientist.

"Bella's a genius." Dominic had his arms around both hourglass waists. "She's in charge of cosmetics research. She's going to make everyone in the world beautiful."

Bella's face heated further. Apparently he also felt the need to excuse her dullness.

"Would you like to join us?" She spoke up, her voice a little squeaky. She knew Dominic would rather be with them than her.

Dominic's smile disappeared and he lifted a brow at her.

"We can't, darling!" The redhead seized the opportunity to kiss his cheek again. "We're just passing through on the way to tonight's party."

"They're event planners," Dominic explained. "They love to serve my products and pretend they paid a fortune for them."

The cream-dress girl leaned toward him. "Don't tell anyone how much you charge for the mushroom pâté." Her French accent gave her words an air of sexy conspiracy. "The hostess is crazy for it. She thinks we buy it from Paris by the ounce."

"It'll be our secret that it's two-fifty for a half-pound tub." Dominic's dimples showed. "I doubt one of your clients would ever go into an actual store, anyway. They have 'people' for that."

The two beauties threw their heads back in musical laughter.

Bella took a bracing swig of her champagne. She'd seen his

stores here and there—Trader Dan's, was that the name?—but had never actually been in one. Apparently she'd been missing out.

She was in danger of shrinking out of existence altogether when both girls chimed, "Must fly!" They kissed him on both cheeks, then back on the first one. Three kisses. Each.

Bella managed to keep a poker face.

"You have lipstick on your cheeks," she said, as the goddesses stalked off toward the door.

Dominic shrugged. "Occupational hazard. I bet you know the best way to get it off."

"The fresh mayonnaise would work, but it might clog your pores. I'd go with the napkin if I were you."

Dominic scrubbed at his chiseled features with the white linen. "Better?"

"Much. I've never seen someone kiss three times before. It gets messy."

"That's how they do it in Europe. There it's just like shaking hands. You get used to it."

"I'll bet. Anyway, I must get going too." She stood. "It's been lovely." She gulped. "The food, I mean."

His eyes narrowed slightly.

She blinked. "And the company, of course. Very nice to meet you, Mr. Hardcastle."

"Dominic." His tone chastised her. He stood and slid his hand into hers. "I'm offended that you're abandoning me here."

"I'm afraid I have a train to catch." She tried to release her hand, but he tightened his firm but gentle hold on it. "I need to visit my mother."

His espresso-shot eyes fixed on hers. "Family's important."

"Yes. Well, I'd better be going." She tugged at her hand again. He didn't release it.

"No way you're leaving without a traditional European

goodbye kiss. That would add insult to injury." He tilted his head. His dark eyes glittered.

Deep breath and get it over with. She leaned forward. The warm salty musk of his skin assaulted her as he lowered his head and pressed his cheek to hers. She kissed the air by his ear and tried to ignore the strange shivery sensation in her arms and legs.

Was he really going to kiss her on both cheeks? A swift movement of his head confirmed her suspicion. She held her breath as his lips brushed her other cheek and a shimmer of desire rippled inside her belly.

She was about to step back and gulp air when she remembered the other girls had kissed three times. Ugh. So pretentious. But she could handle it. Hang tough. She lowered her eyes for the return journey to cheek number one. Braced herself against his male scent. She was almost out of here.

Then something went very, very wrong.

Two

She never knew quite what happened, just that Dominic's mouth collided with hers.

Not a hard, fast kind of impact where things bounce apart.

A slow crash.

The landing soft, warm and quietly devastating.

It was impossible to say what really went on without a photon microscope to analyze activity at the nanometer level.

Something happened, though.

Parted in astonishment, their lips seemed to fuse. Then their tongues touched, sparking a sharp jolt of rogue energy.

A firm hand on her back steadied her and pulled her close, which only made their lips weld more tightly together.

A sizzling—or was it a shivering?—sensation rippled through her limbs, rendering them limp and almost useless. His mouth became her source of strength, infusing her body with energy that raced along her synapses, stinging them to a new level of awareness.

At some point her eyes closed, but this strange new world wasn't dark. Lights and colors flashed in her brain, echoing the dazzle of sensation that engulfed her body.

Confusion and disorientation made her reach and grab for something—anything—to hold on to. That's how her hands ended up under his jacket, fisted in his thick cotton shirt. Gripping, hanging on for dear life.

And then it was over.

She managed to step back, gasping for breath, blinking in the horrible brightness of the restaurant's stark lighting.

Her lips tingled, flushed with blood. Her heart banged against her ribs.

To give him credit, Dominic looked slightly stunned too.

She checked the buttons of her shirt with a shaking hand, anxious to see if they were still closed over her heated and hypersensitive breasts. All in place.

She checked her hair. Still on her head. She forced out a little laugh. "Goodness, that continental kissing is dangerous."

She cursed herself for sounding like such a geek. He probably smooched women goodbye all the time.

It was her problem if her life was so dull that a simple kiss had knocked her right from one dimension into another.

"Well, well, well." Dominic's dark eyes roamed over her face. "You're full of surprises."

Heat crept up her neck. Did he think this was her fault? Could he see her nipples, peaked to hard points, through her blouse? She resisted the urge to look down.

"I prefer a simple handshake," she stammered.

"Not me." Humor shone in his eyes. "I could get used to

goodbyes like that. Maybe I'd better walk you downstairs so we can say goodbye again."

She grabbed her pocketbook off the floor. "Please, don't trouble yourself. Stay and have dessert and coffee."

She needed to get away from this guy. Her recent scientific research had demonstrated that all kinds of strange things could happen in the right circumstances. Unpredictable things.

Dangerous things.

Surfaces could shift and alter their appearance. The very substance of something could fundamentally alter.

Perhaps under the right conditions—the penetrating laser stare of his eyes, for example—her clothes could entirely vanish.

His eyes had turned completely black. Desire radiated from them like heat rising off tarmac.

"Thanks again!" She cleared her scratchy throat. Dominic hadn't moved an inch. "Must fly!"

It was unlikely she could have exited the dining room faster if she actually did fly. She ran—literally—for the door, then gasped for breath as she leaned her whole weight on the elevator button outside.

Her body still hummed with stray bursts of heat and rogue flashes of electricity. Her fingertips stung and even her earlobes felt hot.

No doubt there was some quite ordinary scientific explanation for what was happening in her body.

Then again, as her father's daughter, she knew there was nothing ordinary about science and the miracles and magic that were waiting to be discovered if you dared to dream and venture into the unknown.

She gulped.

Ping.

She dove into the elevator as soon as the doors opened, cutting a swathe through a group of Japanese businessmen. "Sorry!"

She pressed herself against the burled walnut panels as the door closed.

Dominic Hardcastle.

She shut her eyes and willed her body to come under control. She'd locked lips with *the boss's son*.

Was this some kind of game to him? Revenge for the way she'd imperiously ordered him out of her lab?

Did he say he was staying? Would she have to see him every day? Her breath came in ragged gasps.

She wasn't sure she could stand up to the stare of those unrelenting black eyes ever again. She'd probably dissolve into a column of disembodied atoms.

How predictable of her. Tarrant Hardcastle had secured a reputation as the lady-killer of his generation and no doubt his son had inherited the gene. The DNA that enabled them to use people, suck them dry and toss them aside. She hugged herself against the air-conditioned chill.

When the elevator reached the lobby she didn't get out. Instead she pressed the button for the fifteenth floor.

Back to the lab. To find what she was looking for and get out of here. To secure the rights to her father's research and the chance to continue his legacy, before Tarrant Hardcastle and his wickedly seductive son destroyed her chance forever.

Dominic remained in the restaurant for another half hour. He ate one slice of bittersweet Sacher torte with cream, a profiterole drenched in rich chocolate and a lime cheesecake with fresh raspberries. Yes, he had a sweet tooth.

Three cups of black coffee too.

But nothing seemed to fill the strange hole gaping in his gut.

What the hell had that woman done to him?

The waiter refused his attempt to pay the bill or tip. *Thanks, Dad.* He managed not to laugh out loud.

Where had Tarrant Hardcastle been when his mom was trying to make dinner on a grocery budget of twenty dollars a week?

He'd like to see Tarrant Hardcastle go down on his knees to her and beg forgiveness.

Resentment heated inside him, alongside the desire that tight-lipped scientist had ignited there.

Bella Andrews was one of Tarrant's protégés. Funny how all the employees here were both brilliant *and* attractive. There was something downright creepy about that. Were they all *Stepford Wives* clones?

He caught sight of himself in the mirrored steel finish next to the elevator.

You fit right in.

In his dark, well-cut suit, with his dark, well-cut features—which were obviously inherited from his famous father—he blended tastefully with the scenery.

A mocking laugh fell from his lips as he stepped into the empty elevator. His dad hoped he'd stay and take over?

No chance, Pops.

But he wouldn't be leaving empty-handed either.

He went to hit the button for the lobby, but his fingers disobeyed and pressed the number fifteen instead.

No doubt the lab would be locked for the night.

But when the elevator opened, he stepped out.

The door to the lab was closed, as it had been earlier that day. He tried the handle. Once again, it opened.

The room wasn't nearly as bright as it had been earlier. The overhead fixtures were off and the newly risen moon bathed the lab in silver light through the wall of windows.

Eerie.

He knew he shouldn't be here, but that was part of the thrill. Not his fault if they didn't bother to set the lock.

A sliver of light at the far end of the long room drew his attention. His leather shoes were silent on the polished floor as he crossed the lab, past the moonlit shadows of microscopes, and the racks of glassware. He could hear a rhythmic, mechanical sound. Familiar, but he couldn't quite put his finger on it.

In his Bella-awakened state it made him think of sex. Where was Bella now, with her accusing stare and her prim little mouth?

The answer became apparent as he peered through the crack in the door.

The sound was a Xerox machine.

And Bella.

She'd removed her shoes and stood on stockinged tiptoes, feeding sheets of paper into the machine. The moving beam of light flashed past her body, then the copy spat out with a rhythmic *ka-thunk*.

He stood in the doorway. Silent. Watching.

Bella took the sheaf of fresh copies, folded it, and stuck it into a leather briefcase propped against the machine.

So. The copies were going home with her.

She took the originals from the machine and disappeared through a door on the far side of the room. He heard a metal file drawer opening.

He glanced at the digital face of his watch: 10:28.

What in the heck was she doing here, copying documents in the middle of the night?

She emerged, face bent over a new file, golden-brown hair hiding her features. She shoved a hank roughly behind her ear, pulled out a sheet and scrutinized it.

Then something made her look up.

"Aaaa!" She jerked violently and dropped the file. Papers fluttered in the air and scattered about the small copy room.

Her eyes fixed on his, wide with alarm.

Dominic widened the door opening. "Sorry to startle you."

"Wh—wh—what are you doing here?"

"Watching you."

"Why?" She glanced down at the papers on the floor, as if scanning them for incriminating evidence.

"You make compelling viewing."

Her eyes flashed. "You shouldn't be here at this time of night."

"Says who? It's my dad's company, isn't it?" He leaned against the door frame and crossed his arms. "I'm thinking you're the one who's not supposed to be here."

"Why shouldn't I be here?" she snapped. She crouched and gathered the strewn papers. "They're all out of order now."

"Let me help you." He wanted to get a look at the pages. He picked up the closest one, which was covered in typed formulas.

She snatched it from his hand. Her fingertips grazed his palm and his skin tightened at the reminder of their mesmerizing kiss.

"What are these papers?" He picked up another one. Couldn't make heads or tails of it. He could read a balance sheet upside-down from twenty paces, but chemistry was way out of his league.

"Research. Some reading for the train."

"The midnight train to Georgia? You were running to catch your train nearly an hour ago."

"I missed it. I came back to kill some time."

"We're more than ten blocks from Grand Central."

"I had a lot of time to kill." Her gray gaze stuck him like a steel blade.

"I don't believe you." His words hung in the air.

Her startled expression only enhanced his conviction that she was guilty. Of something.

He decided to push. Maybe just to see how hard she'd push back. "I think you're stealing secrets."

"And doing what with them?" she snapped.

"I don't know that. Yet." He crossed his arms over his chest. He was intrigued by anyone daring enough to risk getting on the wrong side of Tarrant Hardcastle.

She tossed her head and picked up more papers. "I'm just doing my job."

"Then you won't mind me looking at those papers in your briefcase?" Why was he doing this? He wanted to get past the cool scientist demeanor as much as he'd wanted to see what lay under that white lab coat. And he had the strings to tug at it. "I am a Hardcastle, after all."

No need for her to know those pages made as much sense as Cyrillic script to him.

She hesitated, blinking. "I'm not stealing anything."

"Prove it."

Her breath came in hard gasps. He could see her chest rise and fall beneath her silk blouse. He stepped into the copy room, narrowing his eyes against the fluorescent light. "Where are the file cabinets?"

"Why are you doing this?" Her voice was shaky.

Why indeed? Yes, he'd had the uniformed pleasures of being both an altar boy *and* a boy scout, but he couldn't cry morality on anyone going up against Tarrant Hardcastle. With his background, he'd be first in line to fight him with them.

Maybe it was the overbearing way she tried to order him out of her lab and called security on him. He'd spent too much time as a scrappy outsider to appreciate being treated like one now.

One thing was for sure: he certainly wasn't motivated by filial desire to protect the interests of dear old Dad.

He shoved past her into the file room. A long drawer sat

open. "Acquisitions," he read aloud. He stopped and flipped through some files. The folder he picked up was full of letters with another company's letterhead. Negotiations for the sale of proprietary research. "Tarrant buys scientific studies?"

"Yes. It's expensive to do them in-house."

"So why does he need *you*?"

"Change of strategy. He wants to stop buying outside work and leap ahead of the competition by investing in new technology."

"And you're selling all that hard-won research to the highest bidder."

Her face turned white. "I most certainly am not!"

"Then what the hell are you doing?" Some primitive part of his brain prayed she'd come up with a good explanation.

She lifted a hand to tuck her hair behind her ear. With some effort he resisted the urge to see if the movement pulled her blouse tight over her full breasts.

"I'm searching for something," she rasped.

She wanted to say more. Her lips quivered.

He could imagine how they'd feel under his mouth, softening and warming.

He tugged his gaze away and fixed it on her gray eyes.

Bella blinked. "Tarrant stole my father's research. I want it back." She lifted her chin.

He stepped forward. He liked to get close to people when they were under pressure. Something subtle let him know whether they were telling the truth. The smell of their pheromones, maybe.

"Who was your father?"

"Bela Soros."

"Bella, like you?"

"It's a man's name in Hungary, where he's from. He worked his whole life developing formulas that would revolutionize the way we perceive things. He sacrificed everything, poured his

whole self into it. He was this close to realizing his dream...."
She held two slender fingers a hair's breadth apart. "Then
Tarrant Hardcastle bullied him into selling it for a song. Now
he's dead. It's not right!"

Her nostrils flared as her indignation rang off the stark,
white walls and metal cabinets of the file room.

"Tarrant *stole* his work, or he *bought* it?" Dominic narrowed
his eyes. The raw emotion on her face tugged at something in
his chest, but her words didn't add up.

"He paid, but with an insulting pittance."

"How much?"

She tilted her chin at him. "I don't know. I'm hoping to find
out from these files. Tarrant browbeat him into it after hearing
him speak at a conference. My father told him no time and time
again...." She inhaled a shaky breath.

"But Tarrant Hardcastle doesn't take no for an answer."

She didn't say anything.

"How do you know it wasn't much money?"

"Because it's all gone. There should have been enough for
a comfortable retirement. My father always had a good research
or teaching job and we lived well. Now my mother has nothing
and she's in danger of losing their home."

Been there, done that. Sympathy swelled in Dominic's chest.
Tarrant Hardcastle didn't give a rat's ass about the people he
used. Once he was done with them they could live on the streets
for all he cared.

"Don't you earn a decent salary?"

"Yes. It's good."

"Perhaps that's revenge enough?"

Bella tilted her head. Her eyes darkened. "My mother sacrificed a lot so Dad could focus on his work. It's been hard for
her, very hard...." Her lip started to quiver and she bit it.

"And how do you plan to get money from Tarrant, now that he already bought the research?"

"It's not only about the money. It's about my dad's legacy. I'll prove Tarrant forced my father into selling against his will and then the courts will restore his work to my family."

Alarm mixed with amusement made him snort. "You're going to sue Hardcastle Enterprises?"

She held his gaze, her gray eyes unblinking. "Yes. I know a judge will do the right thing."

"Sounds to me like you have way too much faith in the legal system and not nearly enough in Tarrant's utter ruthlessness. Did you find what you need?"

She swallowed. "Not yet. Are you going to have me fired?" Her lips pressed together.

"Me? Oh, yeah, the son and heir. I don't know what the hell I'm going to do with you."

Kiss you again, maybe.

"I know I'm close. I've been through nearly all the files. I'll probably find it tonight, then you'll never have to see me again."

"You think I should just let you get away with this?" He tilted his head.

"If you believe in justice." Her gaze dared him to challenge her.

"I'm a businessman. I believe in profits."

It would be only too easy to take her side against Tarrant Hardcastle. If it wasn't for his knack for business, his own mother would still be struggling.

Still, her deceit intrigued him. "You worked here a whole year to get to this point?"

She licked her lips, a hesitant flick of the tongue which sent a shiver of lust to his groin. "The files used to be stored off-site. It took a few months to get them moved here."

"You haven't answered my question. Did you take this

position, work here all this time, taking Tarrant's money—just so you could gather evidence for a lawsuit?"

"I've performed my duties to the best of my ability."

"Apparently you've done a damn good job of it. Tarrant thinks the sun shines out of your ass."

She blinked at his crude expression. At least something rattled her. Her cold-blooded deception appalled him—and intrigued him.

She straightened her shoulders. "We've made a lot of progress."

"You are one cool customer. How can you sit in meetings with the man when you're planning to sue him?"

"It's not personal. It's a matter of business."

Indeed. He could hardly point the finger of accusation. He'd come here with his own agenda: to take back something that Tarrant stole—even though he technically bought it—from him.

He leaned in the doorway of the file room, crowding her. Looked down on her from his six-foot, two-inch vantage point. "Maybe we can make a deal?"

Bella's heart thumped so hard she could hear the blood pounding in her skull.

Was she an idiot?

She should have made something up. A little white lie to send him off course. Now that she'd told him the truth he could go back to his father and Tarrant could prepare his vast legal staff for warfare.

A "deal"?

She frowned. "What do you mean?"

"I agree not to rat you out, you agree to…" He tilted his head and narrowed those pitch-dark eyes.

Her nipples swelled against the smooth nylon of her sturdy, practical bra. She swallowed hard.

"What?" she choked out.

His low chuckle rumbled through the tension-heavy air. She became acutely conscious of how much taller than her he was. A good eight inches, especially with her standing here like an idiot in her stocking feet.

"I've noticed Tarrant only hires beautiful women. Why is that?"

"He's always concerned about the company's image."

Dominic crossed his arms over his broad chest. "Likes to have everyone around him fit the 'brand'?"

His penetrating gaze made her painfully conscious of her blunt-cut hair and well-upholstered body. "I'm not sure why he made an exception in my case."

"Trust me. No exception was made." A dimple appeared in his right cheek. "I guess he's only getting what he asks for when he hires staff because of their looks rather than their reputation." He frowned. "Where'd the name Andrews come from? Are you married?"

She saw his eyes flick to her left hand. "No! Do you think I'd have kissed you if I was married?"

"I have no idea what you'd do, sweetheart. Especially since we've established that you're here under false pretenses."

She sucked in a breath. "Andrews is my mother's maiden name. My name is Bella Soros, almost exactly like my dad's. Tarrant wouldn't have hired me if he knew that."

"How do you know he wouldn't have been delighted to have you continue your dad's work?"

"My mom approached Tarrant when my father was sick. She asked him if my dad could come work here. She was so sure that being back amongst his tools and test tubes would give him the strength to recover. Tarrant told her to get lost."

"Sounds like my loving father all right."

Something in his expression lit a thin ray of hope in her heart. "So you understand?"

Dominic tipped his head back, studied her down the length of his proud nose. "Sure. I understand. I'm not saying I approve." He raised an eyebrow.

All she needed was another few days. Since the files had arrived she'd been combing through them every free moment when no one was around. She only had two more drawers to search. She'd xeroxed at least a thousand pages of her dad's decades-long research to prove the extent of the intellectual property Tarrant swindled him out of. All that remained was to find the amount he'd been paid. Her impractical father and flighty mother had kept few of their personal financial records.

"But you'll keep my secret." Her voice was barely a whisper.

"Like I said, we can make a deal." His dark eyes drifted over her face. Grazed her lips and roamed over her neck. Her skin heated.

He wants to sleep with you.

She could read it in his face as clearly as if he'd said it.

Maybe he was one of those men who just had to conquer every woman that crossed his path? Tarrant Hardcastle was rumored to be such a man, though his terminal illness—not to mention his very young and beautiful third wife—had put a damper on his womanizing ways.

Bella had worked here for a solid year. Smiled in the face of the man who'd destroyed—who'd *killed*—her father. But she had her reasons. Surely she could go one extra step to safeguard everything her mother loved so dearly.

Her fingers and toes stung with panic. She'd come too far to lose it all now. If she could keep him quiet for a few days she'd be done.

Do it.

She took a step toward him and tilted her face upwards. Held her breath as she offered her mouth to him.

One dark brow lifted.

Had she read him wrong?

Her answer came when his lips crushed hotly over hers.

The breath evaporated from her lungs. His big hand settled crudely on her backside and he tugged her close enough for her breasts to wrinkle his starched shirtfront.

Dominic didn't smell like the expensive cologne they sold downstairs. His scent was raw—rough and feral—the aroma of undiluted lust.

His tongue grazed her teeth and sent a shiver of sensation to her toes. Bella found herself on tiptoe, reaching up to deepen the kiss as he craned his neck down to meet her. Her legs trembled from the strain and from the breathless wave of desire that washed over her.

He pulled back first. Simply lifted his head and left her standing there, lips angled toward the recessed light fixture in the ceiling.

She flushed and slammed her lips together.

Dominic's dimples were strangely absent. And something glittered in his near-black eyes.

"Gosh. I must go. My train." Her words trickled out like drips from a faucet. Her brain seemed to have seized up.

She lunged for her briefcase.

"Not so fast, princess. It's dark out. I'll get you a cab."

"I prefer to walk."

"Then I'll walk you."

Dominic guided her out of the lab with his palm. Her walk reflected her personality: prim, elegant, guarded. They didn't speak a word in the bright elevator. She held her head in profile to him, her kissed lips still red.

"Maybe we can make a deal?"

She'd thought he meant to bargain with sex.

He battled the smile that kept wanting to rip across his mouth. How far would she have gone—in that cramped file room—if he'd pressed the point?

She didn't seem like the kind of woman who'd trade her body for a simple promise. A promise he hadn't even offered.

And what a body.

She was slim, but not in the scrawny way of Tarrant's ex-supermodel cohorts. Her long legs were muscled and shapely, her waist an hourglass dip between full, feminine hips and high, rounded breasts.

He couldn't keep his eyes off her curvy rear, and the way the fabric of her fitted skirt shifted over it in rhythmic movements as she strode out of the elevator.

Down boy.

She murmured a polite goodbye to the security guard in the deserted lobby. Dominic took her arm, despite her momentary protest, as they exited to the dark street.

Muggy summer heat lingered in the air. "So you won't tell?" she whispered.

"I've made no promises." He tightened his arm around hers as she tried to pull away. "But I think we're on our way to an arrangement that will work for both of us."

If she'd turned to look at him, the reflected light from the street lamps might have picked out an evil gleam in his eye.

She marched with determined speed, her heels clicking over the pavement. "What time's your train?"

"Eleven-twenty." She didn't turn to look at him.

"You live in Westchester?"

"It's where my mom's house is."

"The house she's about to lose."

"It's a nice house, not big and fancy at all, but the way taxes are these days…" She sucked in a breath. "She has a lovely garden she's put two decades of work into. It would kill me to see her have to give it up."

Dominic glanced at her. Determination strengthened her elegant features. "I think it would take more than that to kill you."

"You don't know me." Her accusing stare made his five o'clock stubble prickle.

"True." He frowned. "Is Tarrant a tough boss to work for?"

"Not really. He leaves me alone to run the lab the way I want."

"He trusts you."

A tiny wrinkle marred her smooth forehead. "Yes. I suppose he does."

"I guess every man's a fool sometimes."

Three

Dominic climbed the marble steps of the El Cubano cigar bar on Fifth Avenue. Tarrant Hardcastle might only have a few months left to live, but he liked to see and be seen. Despite the acres of retail space and plush corporate offices Tarrant owned a few blocks away, he spent a good portion of each day kicking back in his personal armchair at this mecca for the wealthy and self-indulgent.

Without asking, Tarrant had secured him an impossible-to-get membership. Now, although he'd never smoked anything in his life, there was a polished wood humidor with Dominic's name emblazoned on it in engraved gold plate.

Well, the name *Dominic Hardcastle.*

Glittering there among the names of Hollywood bad boys and Capitol Hill big-wigs, that name gave him a stomach-churning dose of mixed feelings.

"Good morning, Mr. Hardcastle. Can I get you a drink?"

He shook his head at the immaculately attired waiter. He didn't need alcohol. His head hadn't stopped spinning since last night, when a brunette scientist with a soft pink mouth and a twisted agenda had knocked him right off kilter.

He'd kissed her again at Grand Central. Fast, hot and hard. Then she ran for her platform and left him there, aching.

He shoved a hand through his hair, tried to dispel the stray energy that cramped his muscles.

"Dominic!" Tarrant Hardcastle held up his arms, as if welcoming the long-lost prodigal back to the fold.

Dominic moved toward him, jaw rigid. He wasn't the prodigal. He was the steady, hardworking son who'd hung in there the whole time, only to have the rules change when he wasn't looking.

"Wonderful to see you, dear boy!"

Tarrant grasped Dominic's hand between both of his. The glowing man-about-town who ornamented the pages of various glossy Condé Nast publications seemed thinner. He'd recently let his hair turn gray, which made him look his sixty-seven years.

"Are you sure I can't tempt you down the road to ruin with one of these magnificent Havanas?" He waved a fat stogie in Dominic's direction. The state-of-the-art ventilation system prevented even a whiff of smoke from straying into the air.

Dominic shook his head. He couldn't help an indulgent smile. It was easy to see how Tarrant's childlike enthusiasm for everything charmed the socks off people around him. "Good, good. Don't want you to get the big C like your old man." Tarrant patted his arm.

His chest tight, Dominic settled into the leather armchair. Floor-to-ceiling windows looked out over the treetops of Central Park.

"So you saw the lab, huh? What d'ya think?"

"Impressive."

"That Bella Andrews is a firecracker. Could have gone anywhere with a research and business background like hers. Zurich, the Mayo—but no, she wanted to come to Hardcastle. Came to me, don't you know?" His satisfied grin revealed two rows of gleaming capped teeth. "Damned fine gal."

Dominic wondered if his father had always talked like an escapee from an Agatha Christie movie, or if his mode of speech was newly adopted to complement the silver hair. He suspected the latter.

"Yeah. She's smart." *Shame she's planning to take you to the cleaners.*

Though whatever she claimed would no doubt be pocket change to Tarrant.

"I can't tell you how much it means to me to have you here." Tarrant wrapped long fingers around Dominic's. "I'm only sorry it took my illness to bring me to my senses. When you're in a certain position, there's a tendency for everyone to want to dip their fingers in your pockets, like they have a right to your hard-earned money. That made me so defensive I pushed away the people who should have meant the most to me."

Emotion thickened his voice and made Dominic look up. Tarrant's blue-green eyes glittered with moisture.

Dominic swallowed. He'd wanted a dad desperately when he was a kid. Other kids had fathers who at least visited them on weekends or sent presents on their birthdays.

Not him.

For years he'd searched the mail for a birthday card, listened for a phone call. He'd imagined himself glancing up during his first communion, or the time his Little League team made the regional finals, always hoping he'd see a tall man standing there watching him.

Never happened.

His mom had told him his father's name, once he plucked up the courage to ask. When he saw an article about Tarrant Hardcastle in the paper one day, he clipped it. He'd stared at the grainy newsprint image of that handsome face, imagining far-fetched reasons why his dad hadn't come to claim him. He even started a scrapbook, gathering information and images to piece together a picture of the father he longed for.

At fifteen, after nursing resentment mingled with painful hope for several months, he'd angrily accused his mother of keeping his existence a secret, at which point she'd sadly and gently told him about the rejected paternity suit and shown him the court papers as proof.

He'd burned his scrapbook in the backyard brazier his mom used for destroying trash. Since then he'd avoided anything to do with Tarrant Hardcastle.

Now that he was grown up and didn't need or want a father any more, he'd turned up.

"I wasn't sure you'd come, you know?" Dominic's heart squeezed as Tarrant patted his hand. "I don't deserve your forgiveness. I know that. I'm not asking for it either. I just want to share what I've created."

Tarrant took a deep breath and lifted his chin. The morning sun played over his weathered skin. "I put my life into this company. Ate, slept and breathed it. It was my child." He fixed Dominic with a shiny stare. "I thought that was enough. To build something and watch it grow."

He took a deep drag on his cigar, then puffed out a ball of smoke which disappeared instantly, sucked out of existence. "It's not enough. Maybe it's because I can't stand the thought that I'm dying. Because I want to hang on and push my way into the future in whatever way I can. But I have to pass it on.

I need a successor to take the garden I've planted and grow it into something even bigger and better."

Tarrant squeezed his hand again and Dominic fought the urge to squeeze back.

"You're the one. You're my heir. Hell, you even look just like me." He slapped the leather arm of his chair with delight. The exertion made him cough a bit.

Dominic looked him right in the face. "I'm not going to be your heir."

"What do you mean? Of course you are! You're perfect. Even a retail entrepreneur yourself. I had no idea that young upstart revolutionizing the way gourmet food was sold was my own flesh and blood. When Sam found you and told me, I couldn't stop laughing. You can't fight destiny, dear boy."

So Tarrant hadn't even recognized his name in the papers. That was a cold splash of reality. Dominic had always imagined his famous father sitting up and taking notice as his stores got raves in the press.

When Tarrant snatched those bankrupt stores out from under him, Dominic had taken grim satisfaction in the idea that at least his father was paying attention to him. Maybe even making some kind of alpha-dog jostle for dominance.

Once again, like the snot-nosed kid with the scrapbook, he'd been kidding himself.

Dominic kept his eyes on Tarrant's. "I came here because I wanted to meet you. I wanted to look you in the face. I wanted to know why you abandoned me and my mom." He inhaled slowly. "I've done that now. I'm glad of the chance to meet you, but I'm not going to take over your company. You don't owe me anything, and I don't owe you anything."

Tarrant's eyes didn't dim. If anything they glowed brighter. "I can see you're a tough customer." He patted Dominic's knee.

"I wouldn't expect anything less. Why should you want to take on a big burden from some old codger who needs a son all of a sudden? Hell, I wouldn't either."

Tarrant leaned forward. "Tell me, Dominic, what can I do for you? For *your* business. I've got my fingers in a lot of pies and I can pull you out a sweet cherry from one. Just say the word."

Here was his opportunity to ask for the stores he wanted. But he'd rather die than take a handout from this man. He should throw his offer back in his face with a stinging insult.

But he couldn't.

Dominic struggled to keep his face emotionless. He'd thought his childish hopes and dreams of reconciliation with his absent father were crushed out of existence and forgotten.

They weren't. They'd been festering away below the surface the whole time and now they bubbled up like acid that stripped his insides raw.

"I've got to go." He stood, burning to be out of this place where anything nasty was sucked out of the air so they could all pretend it didn't really exist.

Tarrant Hardcastle could offer all the gold in his vaults, but that would never change the past.

His clothes felt itchy and uncomfortable as he stepped out into the high-noon heat. His gut churned and his chest ached and his heart kept beating too fast.

He decided to call it lust and go see Bella.

"Hello, Miss Andrews."

Bella started at the deep voice in her ear. *Dominic*. Leaning over her shoulder, staring at the graph in her hand. She snatched it out of sight. "How did you get in here?"

"Through the door."

Kumar and Anita stood not ten feet away, going over some

data in hushed voices. Sue hunched over a microscope at the nearest table, and Theo held a rack of test tubes up to the bright sunlight at the wall of windows.

Dominic's breath, warm on the back of her neck, made her tiny hairs stand on end.

"My research team is here," she hissed.

"I can see that. I look forward to meeting them."

She craned her neck around. His placid, innocent expression warred with the wicked gleam in his eye.

"What do you want?"

"Lunch would work."

She blew out a breath. Anything to get him out of here before he stirred up trouble with her team. "Let's go." She left her report on the counter.

Dominic's eyes widened. Apparently he hadn't expected her to be so easy. To her chagrin, he gestured for her to go first. She deliberately left her lab coat on all the way to the door. She could feel his gaze burning through the white fabric.

"I'll be back in a few," she called, as she hung her lab coat on a hook. She smoothed a hand over the front of the new cream-and-black dress she'd bought on sale. It had called out to her from the window, "Buy me, you know you want to."

It gave her perverse pleasure to buy clothes from anywhere except Hardcastle.

Dominic let out a low whistle as the lab door closed behind them. "Bel-la. The name fits."

His eyes roamed shamelessly over the fitted dress. It had a 1950's-style bodice cut like it was tailor-made for her. The diamond-shaped cutout below the neckline hinted at cleavage but didn't actually show any. Fitted through the waist and hips, the dress flared and fell below the knee.

"Thanks. It's new."

She wanted to smack herself on the forehead the moment the words left her mouth, but his admiring gaze had scrambled her brain.

She'd bought stilettos at the same time. Dominic's lips parted as his gaze drifted over her ankles and feet.

One dark eyebrow lifted very slightly. "If my high school chemistry teacher had looked like you, I might be in a different line of work today."

She shrugged. "Just part of the job. Can't work for Tarrant and be a slob."

His eyes twinkled. "Why does that make me want to change into jeans?"

"I thought you didn't work for Tarrant. Yet. Or did you decide to stay?" Her stomach clenched inside the fitted waistline.

"Any reason why I should tell you?"

"None whatsoever."

The elevator doors opened and he gestured for her to go in first. She couldn't stop her hips from swaying slightly as she stepped over the threshold.

Reality came back with a crunch as the doors closed. She swallowed hard. "Did you tell him about me?"

"No." He leaned against the wall.

A rush of relief made her light-headed. "Thank you."

"Did you find what you were looking for?"

"Not yet." She bit her lip. "It's got to be there somewhere."

"What if it isn't?"

"It is." The door *whooshed* open and several people entered. Dominic's steady gaze heated her skin but she didn't flinch.

On the ground floor he waited until everyone else had left, then offered her his arm. "Where would you like to eat?"

"I usually get a hot dog in the park."

"If eating a hot dog for lunch every day got you that body, I'm not inclined to mess with a good thing."

They pushed out through the revolving door into the sharp midday sunshine. Her new heels clicked on the tarmac as they crossed Fifth Avenue and went into the park. Beneath the thin layer of civility suggested by his expensive suit, Dominic's thick arm held hers tight.

"What do you want with me?"

"We have a deal, remember?" He tilted his chin, enjoying the sun on his face. "Or is breaking your word a habit with you?"

"I've never broken my word."

"Oh, you told my dad you're working against him?"

"I'm not! Well, I want my own father's work back, but I haven't been backpedaling on the science. I'm very proud of what we've achieved."

"But you plan to take it with you?"

"No. I would never take work I've done for Hardcastle. I just want the basic research back. I won't sue for any products I've developed here using it. My dad had no interest in cosmetics. His work had to do with the perception of reality."

"Which I guess can translate into making people appear more trustworthy than they are."

"I can't believe I confided in you."

He looked back at her. "You trusted me."

"Why would I trust you?" She spoke her own question aloud.

"I have that kind of face." His mouth widened into a predatory smile. "Mustard? Ketchup? Sauerkraut?" They'd reached a hot dog cart.

"The works."

Dominic ordered their lunch from a vendor, then led her to a bench in the shade of a large oak. He took a big bite of his hot dog and chewed it. "Tarrant wants me to take over the company. Asked me what I want. He'll give me anything." He took another bite.

Bella frowned. "You mean, like, if you asked for my father's research…" She blinked. Her Diet Pepsi bubbled in her nose.

"The thought did occur to me." He sipped his iced tea.

Her heart squeezed. "Would you do that for me?"

"Nope." He took another bite. Chewed it, inclining his head to the sun again. Light and shade danced over the hard planes of his face and glinted in his black hair.

Bella tried to keep her breathing steady. "Why not?"

"Because if I did he'd figure out who you are and sue your dress right off you for breach of contract."

Her dress tickled her hot skin. "Breach of contract?"

"As an employee you are contractually obligated to support the best interests of the company. What you're doing is no different than a store clerk sticking their hand in the till."

"The only contract I signed was the one agreeing that any scientific discoveries I make here are the intellectual property of Hardcastle. I already told you I don't want to take that."

"Doesn't matter. You came here to take something. You think that's legal? Check your employee handbook." He sipped his tea without looking at her.

Employee handbook? She recalled a thick, red, spiral-bound book she'd filed away unopened. She wasn't planning to run for Employee of the Month.

"Are you saying I can't sue Tarrant, as I will be in breach of a contract I didn't sign?"

"I didn't say a thing." He popped the last piece of hot dog in his mouth and chewed it. His dark eyes never left her face. "Want another?"

"No." She glanced down at her uneaten hot dog. Her appetite had vanished. "So what should I do?" Her voice was shaky.

"You're asking me how to screw over my own dad?" His dimples appeared. "You may look hot in that dress, but I have my limits."

As if to test those limits, he gave her a once-over that threatened to scorch her skin. "Okay, so maybe I'm not sure where those limits are, but I'd give up your Quixotic quest to save the family fortunes if I were you, and enjoy the good gig you have going." He tilted his head. "Perhaps that's what your dad would have wanted."

He said the last part softly. Not a hint of accusation or condescension. The thought turned over in her brain—which instantly rejected it.

"My dad lived for his work. It was everything to him. Without it he felt like an empty shell. He begged Tarrant to allow him to continue it here, but Tarrant wouldn't let him."

Dominic exhaled. "That does sound harsh."

"I guess a white-haired scientist who still wears suits from the nineteen sixties didn't fit his company image." She dropped her unbitten hot dog and its wrapper into her lap. "If he'd just left my dad alone and let him continue his work, I wouldn't be here. I'd be doing my own thing somewhere else. But as it is? I can't. I wouldn't be able to sleep at night."

Dominic looked at her steadily. "Regaining his research won't bring your dad back."

But it could bring my mom back.

She swallowed. "I know that. But to know his work is in safe hands, that it won't be forgotten, that's priceless to me."

She held out her hot dog. "Here, you have it. I've lost my appetite."

She placed it in his wide palm and his fingers closed around it.

"I'm not letting you go back to work until you eat something."

She shrugged. "Hot dogs aren't good for you, anyway."

"Come on." He stood and tugged her to her feet. "I'm taking you somewhere for a real lunch." He tossed the hot dog in a wastebasket and strode for the park exit. Her hand imprisoned in his, she hurried to keep up.

Ignoring her protests, he hailed a cab as soon as they stepped onto the sidewalk, then almost pushed her into it.

"Where are you taking me?" She slammed down on the vinyl seat, gasping for breath. She didn't hear what he said to the driver.

Dominic eased his big body in next to her. The fine wool of his suit brushed her bare arm. "You'll find out soon enough."

"How do I know you're not going to keep me a prisoner in your hotel room?"

Why had that image sprung to mind? And why did it trigger an alarming shiver of anticipation.

She glanced at the cab driver to see if he had rescuer potential. His rhythmic head bobbing didn't look to be a good sign. An iPod earphone peeked out from beneath his turban. Was that even legal?

"Hmm. Good idea." The dimple nearest her made an appearance. "Except I don't have a hotel room."

"Where are you staying?" She gripped the door handle with an unsteady hand as they headed downtown, weaving back and forth through Fifth Avenue traffic in a way that made her stomach lurch.

"A friend's place."

She wondered if it was a female friend, then cursed herself. What did she care? She was hardly hoping for a relationship with Dominic Hardcastle.

She needed him to head straight back to Miami and her to find the file—ideally today.

This little detour was not helping.

He rolled down the window and inhaled a lungful of exhaust and secondhand cigarette smoke. "Damn. I do miss this city. We lived here until I was ten, then my mom got a job that moved us all over the place."

"Are you thinking of moving back?" Her empty stomach cramped.

"Are you trying to say you'd miss me if I went home?"

"Not in the least."

"I'd miss you." He gave her a long-lashed sideways glance. *Flirt.* "You don't even know me." She ignored the funny feeling in her chest.

"I know you have a beef with Tarrant Hardcastle. That gives us something in common."

"You said he'd give you anything you want. Figure out what you want and ask him for it." His attempt to find common ground with her made her palms sweat. Was he setting her up for something?

"I know what I want." A tiny frown etched his forehead as his gaze drifted over her cheek and chin. "I wonder if Tarrant would give *you* to me if I asked nicely."

She whipped around to face him, her fingers tingling to slap his arrogant, handsome face.

He was grinning.

She fought a bizarre urge to laugh. "Oh, stop it. You have me where you want me because I was stupid enough to blab my whole sob story to you."

"Yeah. You should be more cagey."

"Thanks for the tip."

"Anytime." His black eyes roamed insolently over the front of her dress, where the patterned fabric clung to her breasts.

A sudden stray image assaulted her. His mouth on her breast. His tongue making a dark circle on the silk.

She lifted her head and stared out the window. She could feel her nipples peaked hard inside her bra. Wondered if he could see them.

She wanted to suck in a deep breath but she knew that would only draw her dress tighter over her breasts. "I do have work to do, you know."

"Sure. Rifling through the drawers in my family's business."

"Actually, we have a new product coming out." She wanted to prove that she earned her keep. "Two of my researchers have perfected a powder that creates the illusion of perfectly smooth skin. At first it didn't work because oil in the skin broke it down, so the effect didn't last long on a lot of people. Anita came up with a compound that absorbs oil and now we can offer a twelve-hour guarantee."

Dominic looked politely interested. That irked her. "This stuff is effective enough to cover deep scarring. It will change a lot of people's lives."

"That's great."

"You think it's silly."

"I don't. It's a heck of a lot less silly than most of what Hardcastle tries to foist on its consumers. Though, if they sold you that dress I've got to thank them."

"I bought it at Ann Taylor." She smoothed the skirt and hid her smile of satisfaction.

"You would."

They were stuck in traffic. Dominic still had the window open and a chorus of honks pummeled her ears.

"I bet your dad would be really proud of what you're doing with his work." His tone, warm and intimate, made her breath catch.

"He wasn't interested in cosmetics. I think he'd have loved to work for the military, but they wouldn't hire him."

"Why not?"

"He was politically radical for a while after he came to the U.S. Belonged to some fringe Marxist group. He was out of politics by the time I was born, but I guess the stain lingers in the CIA files."

"That's a shame." His sympathetic look almost affected her. "Maybe you inherited his risky passion for lost causes."

Her back stiffened. "It's not funny."

"I know. That's why I don't want to see you screw up your life over something that can't be changed."

"Did you drag me out of my lab to lecture me?"

"Among other things. Feeding you and kissing you were higher on my agenda, but we seem to have gotten out of order."

He leaned forward and slid the partition aside, tapped on the driver's shoulder and gave him some incomprehensible directions. They headed east on Fourteenth Street.

"Since we're working backwards, can I kiss you now?"

The question was straightforward.

Her answer more so. "No."

Four

Bella's pulse picked up. Would he force her? Hold their "deal" over her head?

His expression serious, Dominic raised his thumb and brushed it gently over her lips. "Shame."

How dare he? Her mouth quivered under his insolent touch.

How would he feel if she reached out and—say—ran her fingers through his hair? His thick black hair was combed back, but a natural wave pulled it into disorder that begged to be "fixed". Her palms tingled.

Bella jerked her focus off him and stared out the window. The cab was taking them into the gridless labyrinth of the West Village. "You still haven't told me where we're going. Wouldn't that be polite?"

"You know by now that I can be quite rude when the occasion calls for it." Humor thickened his voice.

"Why do I feel like I should be calling a cop?"

"Maybe you should be." He leaned forward and muttered something to the driver, who pulled over outside a small brownstone storefront.

She climbed out onto the sidewalk, self-conscious in her smart dress among the jean-clad people perched on the edges of sidewalk planters.

He held out his arm, gallant. Aware of all the eyes on her, she took it. He led her up some concrete stairs. Inside people packed in front of a narrow counter. A chalkboard menu covered the far wall. Delicious aromas wafted in the air and she could hear the clatter of pans.

"Best food in the city." Dominic squeezed her arm in his.

"What kind?"

"Italian, of course."

Of course. And to compound his crimes of arrogance, he ordered for both of them without even asking her what she wanted. Or liked.

Or even if she was hungry. Which unfortunately, she was.

He chatted with the guy behind the counter as if they were friends, but didn't introduce her. "Let's sit outside."

Of course, Your Lordship.

"You know, you *are* a lot like Tarrant." She arranged her skirt on the hard bench that ran under the storefront window. "You do everything you damn well please and don't care what anyone else wants."

"There's a lot to be said for being decisive."

"In business, yes, but it can be hard to take in personal relationships. Look how many times your dad has been married."

That got his attention. Dominic's lips pursed like he was about to say something. Then he looked thoughtful. "How many times *has* he been married?"

Regret rippled through her. She'd forgotten that Tarrant was a virtual stranger to him. She probably knew his father better than he did. "Samantha is number three. Have you met her?"

"Yes. Seems nice." He uncapped a bottle of San Pellegrino and poured her a glass. "Young."

"I think she's my age."

Dominic blew out a short breath. Shook his head. "Why would any man want to marry a woman less than half his age?"

"Are you kidding? I thought all men wanted that. Besides, maybe I'm actually fifty, with really great skin."

He chuckled. "Nah. If you were fifty you'd be tougher."

"I am tough!"

He swallowed a draught of the sparkling water. "Yes. You kind of are. I like that."

His smiling friend appeared with two steaming plates of lasagna.

"As good as Mama's?" she asked, once he'd gone back inside.

Dominic leaned toward her. "Not quite, but don't tell Alfie that. He might cry. You know how emotional we Italians get."

"Yeah. Right." Dominic Hardcastle was as emotional as his father's gunmetal Porsche Turbo.

She dug her fork into the thick-layered pasta.

Fast cars, fast women and a fast buck. That's all this type of man cared about. She didn't feel bad about going behind Tarrant's back at all. If she had to play his son's little games, she could do that too.

She knew what was truly important.

Spicy fresh tomato, aromatic ground beef, and basil exploded over her tongue. The pasta was cooked to perfection and the vegetables still crispy. "Mmm. Not bad."

He shot her a long-lashed sideways glance that almost made her lick her lips. But not quite.

A big drop splashed on her nose. She looked up, and another caught her in the eye.

"It's raining."

Everyone grabbed their plates and glasses. Bodies crowded into the tiny storefront, which had only standing room at a counter.

Dominic hadn't budged. Black dots of rain marred the smooth gray wool of his suit. "The apartment I'm leasing is in the building next door." He gestured toward a brick building with a nod of his head. "We'll go up."

Will we, indeed? She opened her mouth to protest, but a thunderclap bruised her eardrums and rattled windows in nearby buildings. A flash of lightning floodlit the darkening sky. She shivered.

"Bring the water," he commanded, as he seized both their plates and marched away.

She picked up the bottle and glasses from the bench. Shook her head, which was getting wet, and followed.

He held both plates deftly in one large hand while he opened a plain metal door with a key. He motioned for her to go first.

She dove through the door out of the rain. "Phew. I wasn't in the mood to get drenched." Goose bumps rose on her skin. From the cool raindrops, of course. Not from anticipation of what might happen next.

"I think that dress would look good drenched."

"It might shrink."

"Yes." A gleam lit his eyes like the eerie lightning outside.

"You *are* evil."

"Shame you're all alone in a strange building with me." He led the way up the stairs. "I hope the power doesn't go out."

Why could she envisage those dimples so clearly when she was behind him?

Bella paused and shook her head, then she followed. She felt safe with him, which was totally ridiculous. She usually had good instincts about people, and she had no reason whatsoever to trust Dominic Hardcastle. He had her between a rock and a hard...

Whatever.

They walked past the row of metal mailboxes not unlike those that ornament the hallway of every walkup in Manhattan. They crossed the old black-and-white tile floor and mounted the standard-issue scuffed marble steps. Weird that a man so wealthy would stay in an ordinary rundown tenement building.

He unlocked a battered door on the second floor and ushered her in.

"Whoa." Inside, the space contradicted every expectation. They stood on a landing with only a minimalist railing where the floor dropped away in front of them to reveal three open stories of space.

A skylight in the roof flooded the tall interior with the spooky half light of the thunderstorm.

"Let's go up." Dominic led the way up a half-spiral staircase rising toward the skylight. She gripped the glasses and bottles, trying not the think about vertigo.

They arrived on a wide platform. White ultramodern furniture gathered around a sort of indoor fire pit.

"The ultimate bachelor pad."

"Yeah. And since my pal who owns it now has a three-year-old and an eighteen-month-old, it's available pretty much whenever I want it."

"Definitely doesn't seem like a good space for kids."

"Not unless they're wearing rappelling equipment. But he designed it himself and he can't bear to part with it. I think it's kind of weird to take a perfectly good building and scoop it out like a tub of ice cream."

He put their plates down on a low table near the fire pit and settled into a wide, white chair. He shrugged out of his jacket.

Rolled his sleeves over thick forearms. He glanced at her. "Go on, eat."

"Stop telling me what to do."

"It pains me to see good food grow cold. I guess because food is my business." He tilted his head and fixed those dark wicked eyes on her. "Pretty please."

She scowled at him, trying not to smile. Picked up her plate. "How did you get into selling food?"

"I like to feed people. It's that nurturing thing."

Yeah, right. She peered at him. "I guess food never goes out of style."

"Nope, and it hurts my soul that processed junk is cheaper and easier to buy than real food. I'm working to change that."

"And make a profit."

"Sure, or I wouldn't be in business." He took a bite of lasagna. "My goal is nothing less than world domination." His relaxed expression suggested he almost took it for granted.

"Like father, like son." She eyed him cautiously.

"We do seem to have a lot in common." He put down his fork. "Including a taste for beautiful and difficult women."

Dominic loosened his collar with a finger. Bella's wary gaze drove him crazy. She was only here because she was afraid he'd spill her secret. She was trying to play him.

That should make him mad.

This girl thought she could swindle Tarrant Hardcastle out of research he'd paid for and distract her enemy's son with a few fluttering eyelashes?

He should teach her a lesson for making that kind of mistake.

He'd already warned her off. Told her she was looking for trouble and likely to find it. But she didn't back down, or even pretend to.

She stared at him again through those gold-tipped dark lashes. Her gray eyes so calm, cool. A perfect industrial spy—except that she didn't seem able to tell a lie.

What other secrets was she hiding, that she might spill if he just asked the right question?

A crash of thunder shook the old building, and a blast of lightning brightened the open space of the apartment. Dominic put down his plate. He'd lost his appetite for food.

She'd refused his kiss, but her lips had swollen and trembled under the pad of his thumb. He suspected he could stimulate a similar reaction in the rest of her body.

He did love a challenge. The prospect of licking her skin—aroused, hot and salty with exertion—made his mouth water.

"Would you like some wine? My friend has a good cellar left over from his partying days."

"I don't drink during the day."

"Very sensible." He took her plate from her lap and put it on the table. She hadn't taken a single bite since they came here.

He had an irrational urge to throw Miss Cool and Controlled a curveball. "Have you ever been in love?"

She blinked. "No. Have you?"

Her answer surprised him. It ended the line of questioning he'd anticipated, and his own question, thrown back at him, caught him by surprise.

"Sure."

Bella smoothed the skirt of her dress "Did she make you so suspicious of women? I bet she broke your heart."

"I'm not suspicious of women. Half my employees are women."

"Perhaps you snoop around trying to figure out what *they're* up to as well."

"I don't. Something about you raised a red flag."

She pursed her lips. That irresistible cupid's bow crimped into two sharp points. "Maybe I remind you of the woman you used to love?"

"No." He shifted in his chair. "You're nothing like her."

She leaned forward. A slight frown marred her perfect skin. "Why else would you pay attention to a nondescript chemist when you're in a twenty-story building packed with the world's most beautiful women? Was she a scientist too?"

Irritation prickled under his skin. "She's a doctor now."

The hint of a smile played about her lovely mouth.

"Hey, I haven't seen her in years. I barely remember her." He undid another button at the neck of his shirt. The AC wasn't turned up enough.

"I don't believe you. I bet you were engaged, weren't you?"

He frowned. "Why do you care?"

"Just curious. I have a feeling about you."

"I hope it's a sensual feeling." He tilted his head.

Her eyes narrowed. "It's a feeling that you're the kind of man who'd cherish his first love and place her on a pedestal."

"I'm Italian."

She smiled. "Only half, apparently. You're going to have to come up with another excuse."

"Okay, so I loved her. I was crazy about her. I wanted to marry her and have babies with her. That what you wanted to hear?"

Her impudent expression slipped a little. "How long were you together?" she asked quietly.

"Five years."

Her eyes widened. "Wow. That's a long time. What happened?"

He tilted his head and stared at her. "That's my business." He got up from the chair and strode across the platform to adjust the AC. He was starting to sweat.

He'd loved Patricia's sharp mind as much as her lush body.

Her dream of being a doctor had excited him and he'd done everything he could to help her—paying for their apartment while she was in school, bringing home the groceries—all while struggling to get his business off the ground.

She wouldn't marry him until she'd graduated, and he'd had that date engraved on his heart.

Then, two weeks before she was due to pick up her diploma, she announced she was taking a residency in California and would be going alone. She wanted a high-octane career, not the demands and responsibilities of a family.

He was glad the gloom of the storm hid his expression. Since then he'd concentrated his energies on his own business. He didn't need anyone else to complete his life.

He heard Bella get up from her chair. "I'm sorry. It was rude of me to pry. I'd better get back to the lab."

"Of course. You have an *agenda*." He couldn't keep the edge out of his voice.

"Yes." Her lashes lowered to hide her eyes as she smoothed a wrinkle in her dress.

Desire flared in him at the way the fabric clung to her rich curves. She'd worn that dress to attract attention. To arouse.

"Do you get pleasure from tormenting men?" He stepped closer to her. He could smell her skin, warm and sweet.

"I…no." Alarm shone in her eyes. She blinked.

The lightning and thunder had stopped, but the dim half-light of the overcast sky enveloped them in shadow. A ray of sun pierced a cloud and shot down to divide the air between them.

She looked away, as if searching for something. The light caught her cheekbone, high and sharp, highlighting the satin sheen of her skin.

She said something, but he couldn't make out the words because his attention was too intently riveted on her mouth. The sharp angles of her upper lip and the soft pink fullness of the lower absorbed him completely.

The shaft of sunlight glanced across her face and she blinked, squinting. She raised her hand to shield her eyes and the action pulled her dress tight over her breasts and across her slim waist. "I said, should we bring back the plates?"

"No."

She didn't struggle. Not even a little, the way he realized later that she should have.

That would have stopped him.

Instead she surrendered completely, with a shuddering sigh that sealed the inevitability of what was about to happen.

They didn't even kiss right away. He buried his face in her neck, inhaled the mesmerizing scent of her skin. She pressed her cheek to his, her hands fisting into his hair, clutching at his shirt.

His breath came harder and faster, but he couldn't do anything about it. His fingers pushed into the skin of her back through the delicate fabric of her dress, seeking her warmth and the soft femininity of her lush body.

He chafed his palms over her curves, up and down her spine and past her waist. Her ragged breath heated his skin and stirred the rage of desire roaring through him.

He unzipped her dress with a sure, fast swipe and pushed it back over her shoulders.

Why her? Why now?

Her deception and her unrepentant attitude irked him for reasons he couldn't articulate. She wouldn't listen to reason. Was it irritation that heated his blood?

The thoughts pushed through his brain even as he sank his hot, hungry mouth over her breast, suckling it through her bra.

But none of those things explained his reaction to this woman. Was she going along just to keep him quiet? Sex as blackmail?

He didn't care. Couldn't help himself.

Her fingernails scratched him as she struggled with the buttons of his shirt, then gave up, tugging at it and trying to pull it over his head.

A low moan squeezed from her throat. He trailed his mouth over her belly button and shoved her dress down with one hand. He licked, hungry for the taste of her, for the warmth of her skin against his.

He cupped her buttocks with both hands, their full shape driving him crazy. He could feel her fingers in his hair, holding tight, tugging his head back until she bent to kiss him and their mouths tangled together in a hot and breath-stealing kiss.

He never did know what happened to his clothes. Maybe he'd forgotten to wear a belt and his pants just fell off. All he could remember was the sensation of her slim, cool fingers reaching under the cotton of his boxer shorts, taking hold and driving him into a state of madness he never really came back from.

He struggled with the condom he'd scrambled to find in the bathroom. Her fingers worked over his skin, teasing and taunting him, driving him further and further into a fog of lust.

He let his mouth roam over her naked body, inhaling the rich female scent of her skin until he wondered if he'd lose his mind altogether.

Then she climbed over him with trembling thighs and welcomed him inside her.

Bella slid her hips down and took him deep. She couldn't stop the moan of pleasure that issued from her lips. Lips that had trailed over the hard lines of his face, down his neck and along his broad, muscled shoulders.

He sucked hard on her neck, until she could feel his teeth against her skin. Heat surged through her, stung her fingers and toes and made her buck against him.

The boss's son.

This was the kind of mistake that ended careers. That ruined lives.

He laved her nipple with his tongue, which made her cry out and arch her back, shivering from head to toe.

His big hands held her waist, gripping her, his palms on her backside and his thumbs against her belly, and she couldn't help but wriggle against him.

Then he buried his face between her breasts, a gesture so intimate and tender it almost broke her heart.

She didn't realize how much she'd missed simply being close to someone.

Dominic's broad palms slid over her back, sparking fire under her skin. His arms closed around her and made her rock her hips and pull him even deeper into her until the sensation became almost too intense to bear.

She was a scientist. She studied things, tried to understand them, but she didn't understand these feelings surging through her. She couldn't control them any more than she could stop breathing.

Dominic's strong hand cupped her face and tipped it to meet his. Her eyes opened for a split second and she took in the expression that tightened his handsome features. Then his mouth covered hers, greedy with passion.

She couldn't prevent her hips from kicking into a steady rhythm that sent ripples of pleasure shocking through her.

Their tongues fought and their arms wound around each other. The rhythm heightened, gathering intensity. Emotion built inside her until she thought she might burst, or cry, or cry out with the painful fullness of it.

It's just sensation. It doesn't mean anything.

She was just using him. Trying to distract him.

Wasn't she?

Dominic's strong arms held her so tight they almost squeezed the breath from her lungs. They felt so good wrapped around her, so *safe*. She'd been tired and lonely and scared for so long, and sometimes she couldn't remember what it felt like to feel any other way. She didn't want him to ever let go.

Even though she wasn't safe at all.

Strange guttural sounds rose from her throat and mingled with his low, throaty groan as the rhythm rose to a crescendo. Her hands clutched at him, trying to get a grip, to hold on tight.

She was losing it, losing the ability to think or even feel. Then he gathered her in his arms and gave a last hard thrust that pushed her over the ragged edge of reality.

It was a high edge, and she fell and fell and fell, reaching and grasping but finding nothing to grab on to on the way down. She knew the landing would hurt. That she'd fall hard and fast and possibly be bruised, or maybe even crushed beyond repair.

And she was right.

Five

Two hours later Dominic shoved through the revolving doors of Hardcastle Enterprises, irritation and lust still burning on his skin and in his blood.

He was disgusted with himself. He'd taken advantage of a vulnerable woman who knew he had the power to destroy her.

He was disgusted with Bella too. If she'd put up even the slightest hint of resistance he would have stopped. Was she so afraid of him, of his relationship to Tarrant, that she didn't dare say no?

She'd said no to his kiss in the cab.

Then again, he'd said no to his father's offer of the company, or any of its juicy component parts. That didn't mean he didn't want them. He just didn't want to owe Tarrant anything.

He marched across the marble lobby toward the bank of elevators. He itched to own that chain of stores he'd lost to his father. He'd had the future of each store plotted out, right down to the inventory and staffing needs, only to see Tarrant sneak them out from under his nose.

He pushed his thumb hard on the button for the executive floor.

Hardcastle Enterprises didn't seem to have any plans for the stores. Tarrant was just sitting on them like the proverbial dog in the manger. When he was dead, it wouldn't be too hard to convince his successor to part with them.

When he was dead.

His gut clenched. He didn't want Tarrant to die.

The odd realization came as the elevator opened onto the executive office floor.

"Dominic!" Samantha spotted him from where she stood chatting with the receptionist. Tarrant's third wife was younger than he. Her pale blond hair fluttered as she sprang across the carpet and kissed him on the cheek. Only once, thank God.

"Tarrant hasn't stopped talking about you. They're going over sales projections for the next quarter. Totally over my head, I'm afraid, but I know he wants you in there."

Dominic had reluctantly agreed to come to the annual board meeting, and Tarrant was almost tearful with gratitude. His own motivation had been learning insider information about the company that he might exploit to his advantage.

If he felt at all bad about that he just had to recall the memory of his mom cleaning people's houses after work to make ends meet. Removed guilt pangs like Lava soap on grease.

But now he was late because he'd gotten held up screwing a key executive. An executive whose main goal in life was to screw Tarrant over.

"Something came up," he muttered.

Her bracelets jingled as she pressed a hand on his arm. "Oh, he won't mind that you're late. I know he's dying to introduce you to everyone." Her expensive scent assaulted his nose.

"No, I mean I won't be able to make the meeting. A problem cropped up, I need to get back to work."

Her carefully made-up face crumpled. "Oh, Dominic. Please do go in, just for a minute."

He steeled himself against her pleading expression. "I have calls to make."

She grabbed his arm with a force that got his attention. "Come with me." She tugged him down the hall and into an empty conference room. He was too startled to resist. That, and her manicure was close to drawing blood.

In the room she let go of him and put her hands on her skinny hips. A stray image of Bella's glorious full hips crept into his mind and he tried to shove it away.

"Let's not kid around. I know you're probably disgusted that your father not only abandoned you and your mother but now he's married to someone like me. I know I'm young, that people think I'm just a gold digger trying to get rich by marrying a sick man."

Dominic struggled to keep his expression blank.

"I love your father. I really love him. He's made a lot of mistakes but he's a good man." Her eyes grew moist. Dominic braced himself against the possibility of tears, but she seemed to get herself under control. "Nothing matters more to him than finding a successor, and you are the ideal person to take over Hardcastle Enterprises. With your retail background you already have the skill set and the knowledge required to—"

"So he told me. But from what I hear, I'm not Tarrant's only bastard child, so I suspect he'll come up with another heir who fits the bill."

His blood boiled at the reality that other kids had suffered the same treatment as he and his mother. *Let one of them have the company.*

"I know it's an awkward situation. You have every right to

feel bitter about how you've been treated. Tarrant is the first to admit he was wrong. He knows he only has a short time to live and a lifetime of wrongs to right, but he's doing his best."

Dominic scowled. "Wrongs to right? You can't rewrite the past."

"He wants to make amends." She drew in a shaky breath. "He went down to Florida last week to see your mother."

"What?"

"He signed papers affirming paternity, and paid a full eighteen years of inflation-adjusted child support."

Dominic realized his mouth was hanging open and he snapped it shut. "Very useful now, when she doesn't have a child to support."

"He also offered her a million dollars in company stock, but she wouldn't take it."

"I don't blame her."

Anger crackled through his muscles. They didn anything from the man who'd pretended they didn't exist. could take care of his mom now.

"Tarrant will never know what my mom went through trying to raise me alone."

"She did a great job."

Silence hung in the air.

He forced a sarcastic smile. "Gee, thanks."

"You don't have to like me." Her eyes were a fierce blue. "You don't even have to like Tarrant. He certainly doesn't expect you to. But please…"

She grabbed his arm again. The pressure of her fingers and her pleading gaze should have annoyed him, but instead they touched something in him.

"Please at least consider Tarrant's offer. Stay long enough to get to know the company. Hardcastle Enterprises employs thousands of people, all of whom need a strong leader to keep their jobs and livelihoods safe. Go into the board meeting, even if only for a minute. He's a dying man." Her voice rose as she pulled out all the stops, one by one.

Dominic got tired of his heartstrings being played like a harp. "Okay." He could sit through one more meeting to get Tarrant's wife off his case.

She heaved a sigh of relief and a huge smile spread across her face. "Thanks, Dominic."

"He should put you in sales."

She laughed, but she did escort him all the way to the door of the boardroom. Maybe she thought he'd try to make a run for it.

Maybe he would have.

Dominic's muscles cramped as he sat there surrounded by people who breathed, lived and loved Hardcastle Enterprises. Any of the company men and women at the table would probably have been happy to take over the CEO role, and from what he could tell, most of them would have been at least competent. But Tarrant wanted him, because of a blood tie he'd once rejected as meaningless.

Dominic shifted in his chair. He wished he thought it was meaningless, but he knew deep down it wasn't. At least not to him.

If he wanted revenge, he could take over the company then defy his father's wishes by selling it or breaking it up. He could reduce the proud Hardcastle Empire to a handful of dust and memories.

Which, of course, he would never do in a million years. His mom hadn't raised him that way.

Sometimes a deep sense of honor could be a real pain in the ass.

"And nothing makes me prouder than being able to share our best quarter ever with *my son*."

Tarrant's emotion-laden voice boomed along the walnut